THE BANK STREET BOOK OF
MYSTERY

GRAPHIC STORY COMICS ADAPTING THE WORK OF
ISAAC ASIMOV AND O. HENRY
AND OTHER WORLD-FAMOUS MYSTERY AUTHORS

Edited by Howard Zimmerman,
Seymour Reit, and Barbara Brenner

A Byron Preiss Book

POCKET BOOKS
New York   London   Toronto   Sydney   Tokyo

ACKNOWLEDGMENTS

This collection was in every sense a team effort. The editors would like to thank the following people for their contribution to this unique series:

At Bank Street College of Education

Jim Levine, William Hooks, Barbara Brenner, Seymour Reit, Linda Greengrass, Virginia Kwarta, Sam Brian, Lorenzo Martinez and Margaret Peet.

At Byron Preiss Visual Publications, Inc.

Howard Zimmerman, Mary Higgins, Gwendolyn Smith, David Keller, and Ruth Ashby.

At Simon & Schuster

Patricia MacDonald, Jonathon Brodman, Pat Cool, Joanne Goodman, and Mary Frundt.

And finally, our thanks to those authors whose works have been adapted for this series, and to those artists and writers who brought the stories to life.

THE DANGEROUS PEOPLE Copyright © 1989 by Fredric Brown. THE MAN IN MY GRAVE Copyright © 1989 by Edward Gorman. THE LITTLE THINGS Copyright © 1989 by Isaac Asimov. EATS Copyright © by Richard Laymon. WHO? Copyright © 1972 by H. S. D. Publications, Inc. Reprinted by permission of the author. THE GOOD TIMES ALWAYS END Copyright © 1989 by David Morrell. THE DISAPPEARING MAN Copyright © 1989 by Isaac Asimov. THE LITTLE OLD LADY FROM CRICKET CREEK Adapted by permission of the Author and the Author's agents, Scott Meredith Literary Agency, Inc., 845 Third Avenue, New York, NY 10022. THE CURSE OF THE EGYPTIAN TOMB Copyright © 1989 by Nancy Roberts.

Mechanicals by Mary Griffin
Book lettered by Gary Fields

This novel is a work of fiction. Names, characters, places and incidents are either the product of the author's imagination or are used fictitiously. Any resemblance to actual events or locales or persons, living or dead, is entirely coincidental.

Another *Original* publication of POCKET BOOKS

POCKET BOOKS, a division of Simon & Schuster Inc.
1230 Avenue of the Americas, New York, NY 10020

Copyright © 1989 by Byron Preiss Visual Publications, Inc.
Introduction copyright © 1989 by Bank Street College
Cover artwork copyright © 1989 by Byron Preiss Visual Publications, Inc.

All rights reserved, including the right to reproduce
this book or portions thereof in any form whatsoever.
For information address Pocket Books, 1230
Avenue of the Americas, New York, NY 10020

ISBN: 0-671-63148-9

First Pocket Books trade paperback printing September 1989

10 9 8 7 6 5 4 3 2 1

POCKET and colophon are registered trademarks
of Simon & Schuster, Inc.

Printed in U.S.A.

Contents

A Message from Bank Street

Mystery. The word itself makes us think of unexplained events, unsolved crimes and strange twists of fate. There are true mysteries and mysteries that come entirely from the imaginations of talented writers. All of them fascinate us, whether they're in the form of books, plays, TV shows or movies.

Writers seem to enjoy mysteries as much as their audience does. Many literary giants, like Charles Dickens, have tried their hand at the form *(The Mystery of Edwin Drood)*. Other equally famous writers—like Arthur Conan Doyle, Dashiell Hammett and Agatha Christie owe their reputations entirely to the "Whodunit." Edgar Allan Poe is so well known for his mysteries that today's Mystery Writer's Association Award bears his name.

Reading mysteries is a little like eating peanuts. Once you start, it's hard to stop. Some people read every new mystery by their favorite author, and follow the adventures of their favorite detectives the way other people follow the lives of rock stars.

The mystery story form seems to attract people of all ages and from all walks of life. Former President Franklin D. Roosevelt was said to be an avid mystery fan. There must be a good reason why so many people love a mystery. Maybe it's because a mystery is really a puzzle. And humans seem to like to figure out why and how things happen. We like to come up with the answer to a riddle, whether it's who is trying to kill the rich woman, as in our story "Eats," or what is in the strange oblong box, in Poe's haunting story.

In addition to Edgar Allan Poe and O. Henry, this book features stories written by some of today's leading writers of mysteries. Authors like Isaac Asimov, Ed Gorman, Richard Laymon and David Morrell continue to spin mystery yarns that grip and amaze their readers. If you like one of their stories, you can find others by them in your local library. Or, perhaps you will be inspired to write a mystery story of your own. And, who knows? Maybe someday it will be adapted and appear in a book like this one. And then a whole new generation of readers will get a chance to solve a mystery that you have created.

THE DANGEROUS PEOPLE

BY
FREDRIC BROWN

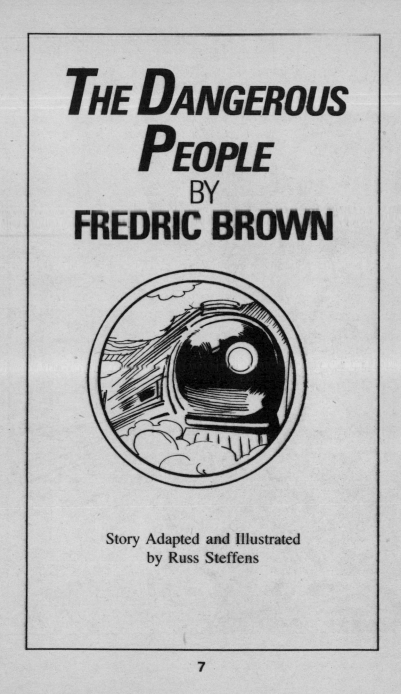

Story Adapted and Illustrated
by Russ Steffens

MR. BELLEFONTAINE SHIVERED A BIT, STANDING ON THE OPEN PLATFORM OF THE LITTLE TRAIN STATION, BUT IT WASN'T FROM THE COLD.

ATLANTIC

IT WAS THE SOUND OF THAT SIREN, BLARING AGAIN -- A DISTANT SCREAM IN THE NIGHT, LIKE FROM SOME POOR TORTURED FIEND.

HE'D HEARD IT FIRST A HALF HOUR BEFORE. THE TOWN BARBER HAD TOLD HIM ABOUT THE NEARBY HOSPITAL FOR INSANE CRIMINALS. AND HOW THE ALARM WENT OFF EVERY TIME AN INMATE ESCAPED.

BELLEFONTAINE HURRIED DOWN THE PLATFORM TO THE DOOR OF THE STATION. HE WAS BREATHING HARD FROM HIS ASTHMA, AND FROM THE WEIGHT OF HIS BRIEFCASE.

THE CASE WAS HEAVY FROM THE GUN HE CARRIED--FOR A FRIEND, ANOTHER LAWYER. AS A FAVOR, HE'D PROMISED TO DELIVER IT TO THE MAN'S BROTHER WHEN HE ARRIVED IN MILWAUKEE.

HIS FRIEND HAD BOUGHT IT AS A PRESENT, BUT WASN'T SURE HOW TO SEND IT. AND, SINCE BOTH HIS BROTHER AND BELLEFONTAINE BOTH LIVED IN MILWAUKEE, HE'D ASKED THE FAVOR.

IT WON'T BE ANY TROUBLE. JUST CALL HIM WHEN YOU ARRIVE AND HE'LL COME PICK IT UP.

THE FACT IS, I ALREADY WROTE TO MY BROTHER AND TOLD HIM THAT YOU'D BE BRINGING IT.

SO THERE REALLY HADN'T BEEN ANY WAY TO SAY "NO" WITHOUT OFFENDING HIS FRIEND.

BELLEFONTAINE PAUSED TO CATCH HIS BREATH AT THE DOOR TO THE STATION. HE WAS OUT OF ASTHMA MEDICINE, AND THE LITTLE TOWN'S DRUGSTORE DIDN'T CARRY IT.

IT WAS ONLY TEN AFTER SEVEN. BELLEFONTAINE WOULD HAVE TO WAIT THIRTY-FIVE MINUTES FOR HIS TRAIN.

THERE WAS ONE OTHER TRAVELER WAITING INSIDE THE STATION.

HELLO. YOU TAKING THE SEVEN-FORTY-FIVE?

YES. THROUGH TO MILWAUKEE.

I GET OFF AT MADISON. WE'VE GOT A COUPLE OF HUNDRED MILES TO GO TOGETHER. MY NAME'S JONES-- BOOKKEEPER FOR THE SAX PAINT COMPANY.

OH. HOW DO YOU DO?

HE SHOULD HAVE SAID MORE, BUT THE TALL STRANGER MADE HIM FEEL UNEASY.

11

12

SUDDENLY, BELLEFONTAINE KNEW WHAT IT WAS. HE REALIZED THAT THE MAN'S CLOTHES DID NOT FIT. THEY WERE MADE FOR SOMEONE SEVERAL INCHES SHORTER, AND MORE THAN A FEW POUNDS HEAVIER.

THE COLLAR OF THE MAN'S SHIRT WAS TOO BIG FOR HIS SKINNY NECK...

...AND HIS EYES WERE ALL BLOODSHOT.

BELLEFONTAINE SAT VERY STILL. OF COURSE, HE COULD BE WRONG. BUT...

DO YOU THINK WE'RE SAFE HERE?

BELLEFONTAINE JUST STARED AT THE MAN... AND HIS CLOTHES. STOLEN CLOTHES, MOST LIKELY--AND MAYBE HE'D HAD TO KILL TO GET THEM. KILLED... A SHORT, STOCKY MAN WITH A THICK NECK.

WHAT'S WRONG? WHAT'S THE MATTER?

13

NOTHING.

THE STRANGER STARED AT HIM. THEN, SLOWLY, HE LOWERED THE POKER.

HE KNOWS I'VE FIGURED OUT THAT HE'S THE ESCAPED MANIAC! IF I WALK OUT OF HERE NOW, HE'LL KNOW I'M GOING TO THE POLICE. HE COULD CRIPPLE ME WITH THAT POKER BEFORE I EVEN REACH THE DOOR.

HE WOULDN'T EVEN NEED THE POKER-- HE COULD STRANGLE ME. AND I'M DEFENSELESS... OR AM I?

BELLEFONTAINE'S EYES DARTED ABOUT IN A FRANTIC SEARCH. HE SAW THE DOOR MARKED "MEN."

BELLEFONTAINE BROKE OUT IN A COLD SWEAT. HE SLOWLY STOOD AND PICKED UP HIS BRIEF-CASE. HE MANAGED TO MAKE HIS VOICE ALMOST CALM AS HE SPOKE--

YOU'LL HAVE TO EXCUSE ME FOR A MINUTE.

THERE WAS A BOX OF BULLETS, ALONG WITH THE GUN.

HE WOULD LOAD IT--BUT HE HAD TO HURRY.

WHAT A NUT-CASE THAT GUY IS. SO NERVOUS... EVEN TOOK HIS BRIEFCASE INTO THE WASHROOM. HE'S DEFI-NITELY OFF HIS ROCKER.

"OF COURSE, I WAS PRETTY CRAZY MYSELF LAST NIGHT, AT MY SISTER'S PARTY."

"I DRANK FAR TOO MUCH. IT'S NO WONDER I COULD HARDLY STAND... DIDN'T EVEN FEEL IT WHEN I FELL IN THE MUD."

16

17

FROM A LONG WAY OFF, THERE CAME THE PIERCING SOUND OF A TRAIN WHISTLE.

OF COURSE! THAT'S WHAT HE'S WAITING FOR -- THE ROAR OF THE TRAIN...

...TO DROWN OUT THE SOUND OF THE GUN!

JONES TIGHTENED HIS GRIP ON THE POKER... AND BELLE-FONTAINE REACHED FOR HIS GUN.

SUDDENLY, THE DOOR TO THE STATION SWUNG OPEN --

GOOD EVENING, GENTLEMEN.

HAVE--HAVE THEY CAUGHT THE MANIAC YET?

NO. AND I DON'T THINK THEY EVER WILL.

HE KILLED A COP IN WAYNESVILLE, STOLE HIS GUN AND UNIFORM.

BUT THE POLICE DON'T EVEN KNOW ABOUT IT YET!

JONES AND BELLEFONTAINE LOOKED AT EACH OTHER, AND SUDDENLY THEY WERE IN MOTION-- ATTACKING THE MAN IN UNIFORM.

THEY HAD BEEN READY TO FIGHT FOR THEIR LIVES. IF THE ESCAPED MANIAC HADN'T ENTERED WHEN HE DID, THEY WOULD HAVE TRIED TO KILL EACH OTHER.

WHEN THE CONVICT CAME TO, THE POLICE WERE ALREADY THERE. DIZZILY, HE REMEMBERED THE TWO MEN ATTACKING HIM-- EVEN THOUGH HE WAS DRESSED AS A COP. WHY, THEY MUST HAVE JUST BEEN WAITING FOR SOMEONE TO KILL.

THEY MUST BE CRAZY.' IF DANGEROUS PEOPLE LIKE THAT ARE RUNNING AROUND OUT HERE, I'M BETTER OFF BACK IN THE HOSPITAL!

THE DANGEROUS PEOPLE
by
Fredric Brown

Fredric Brown's stories use humor to good effect. He was known for his comic tales of people in a mad universe. Born in 1906, Brown wrote books, TV scripts, and short stories. His short story "Madman's Holiday" was adapted as the film *Crack-up* in 1946. He also wrote for the Alfred Hitchcock TV series, and won an Edgar award in 1948 for a story called "The Fabulous Clipjoint," considered by some people to be his best work.

This story sets up an explosive situation. Now that you've read it, ask yourself:

- What would you do in these circumstances?

- Did the author surprise you at the end?

- What does this story say about the idea of "convicting the wrong man"?

THE NAME ON MY GRAVE

BY
ED GORMAN

Story Adapted by Ed Gorman

Illustrated by Robin Ator

IN 1891, IT WAS QUITE COMMON FOR RAILROAD PASSENGERS TO BE DELAYED...

TRACK IS WASHED OUT AHEAD. WE'LL HAVE TO STOP IN MAYFAIR FOR A WHILE...

THE MENTION OF "MAYFAIR" TROUBLED LAWYER ROBERT BANYON. TEN YEARS AGO--BUT NO-- HE DIDN'T WANT TO THINK OF THAT NOW...

24

FOR THE NEXT HOUR AND A HALF, BANYON AND HIS EIGHT-YEAR-OLD DAUGHTER JENNY WALKED AROUND THE CITY OF MAYFAIR.

TO KILL SOME TIME, BANYON TREATED HIS DAUGHTER TO AN ICE CREAM SODA. BUT AS THEY SAT THERE, HE BECAME AWARE OF EYES WATCHING HIM.

SHERIFF VAN FOSTER WAS LOOKING TO SEE IF THERE WAS ROOM FOR HIM TO TAKE HIS AFTERNOON BREAK... WHEN HE SPOTTED A FACE THAT SEEMED FAMILIAR.

--OTHER THINGS AS WELL.

AS BANYON AND JENNY CONTINUED THEIR WALK, THEY WERE APPROACHED BY THE SHERIFF.

SAY-- I'D LIKE TO TALK TO YOU!

YES, SHERIFF?

YOU'RE WAITING FOR THE TRAIN, JUST PASSING THROUGH?

YES MY NAME'S KUBEK! BANYON... I'M A LAWYER. AND THIS IS MY DAUGHTER, JENNY.

PLEASED TO MEET YA, MR. BANYON. I WONDER IF YOU'D TAKE A WALK WITH ME... UP TO THE GRAVEYARD.

"UP FROM TEXAS, THE KID WAS. TRIED TO TURN PEACEFUL, BUT NOBODY WOULD LET HIM, BECAUSE HE WAS KNOWN AS A GUNFIGHTER.

"HE TOOK A JOB AT THE LIVERY STABLE. WORKED AS HARD AS ANYONE.

"HE TRIED TO BE A MODEL CITIZEN.

"BUT NO MATTER HOW HARD HE TRIED, THINGS JUST WOULDN'T GO THE KID'S WAY.

31

"THEN, ONE NIGHT, THE KID TOOK SICK...AND DIED.

"SO, THE NEXT DAY, THEY BURIED HIM. STOLTZ, THE UNDERTAKER, TOLD ME THE STORY. IT HAPPENED BEFORE I GOT TO TOWN, YOU UNDERSTAND."

33

35

FOR THE FIRST TIME IN TEN YEARS, BANYON KNEW HE WOULD SLEEP WELL THAT NIGHT...

...BECAUSE THE LAREDO KID HAD FINALLY BEEN PUT TO REST.

THE NAME ON MY GRAVE
by
Ed Gorman

Edward Gorman has written books in a variety
of fields, most recently *The Autumn Dead* and
Several Deaths Later. In 1988, he won the Private
Eye Writers of America Shamus Award for best
short story. He is also editor and co-publisher of
Mystery Scene magazine. He lives and works in
Cedar Rapids, Iowa, where he runs his own ad-
vertising agency.

This story is in the tradition of "the reformed
rascal" of westerns. Now that you've read it, ask
yourself.

- Have you ever done something you
  couldn't live down?

- What do you think Jenny may be feeling?
  Imagine her thought balloon.

- Would you have acted as the sheriff did?
  Why or why not?

THE LITTLE THINGS

BY
ISAAC ASIMOV

Story Adapted and Illustrated
by Rick Geary

39

40

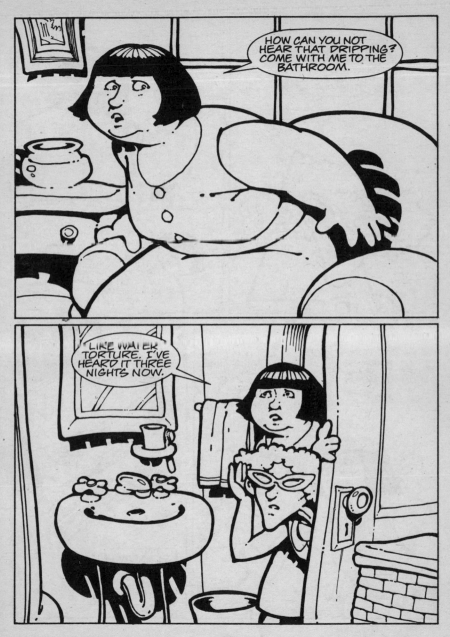

41

42

43

44

"I WATER HER PLANTS WHEN SHE'S OUT OF TOWN, AND HER PLACE LOOKS NORMAL."

THEN YOU HAVE THE KEYS?

YES, BUT I CAN'T JUST GO IN.

WHY NOT, HESTER? YOU HAVE TO WATER THE PLANTS.

SHE DIDN'T TELL ME TO.

MAYBE SHE'S SICK IN BED AND DIDN'T ANSWER THE DOOR.

SHE WOULD STILL ANSWER THE PHONE.

SHE COULD BE DEAD... A HEART ATTACK OR SOMETHING.

BUT SHE'S SO YOUNG AND HEALTHY LOOKING.

46

48

THE LITTLE THINGS
by
Isaac Asimov

Isaac Asimov came to the United States from the U.S.S.R. when he was three years old. He wrote his first original story when he was eleven. Later he earned a degree in biochemistry and taught in a university. Considered one of the great science-fiction and mystery writers of today, Asimov has written more than 320 books on various subjects related to science, including *The Fantastic Voyage*. He is known for his compulsive work habits, which include nine-hour working days seven days a week.

Now that you've read this story, ask yourself:

- Why do you think the author set his scene in such an *ordinary* apartment?

- What purpose does the button serve in this story?

- Have you ever had an experience in which someone wasn't whom you thought he was?

*E*ATS
BY
RICHARD LAYMON

Story Adapted by Mark Borax

Illustrated by Lee Moyer

51

IT WAS *DREADFUL*. ONE MOMENT HE WAS COMPLAINING THAT THE HOLLANDAISE SAUCE HAD CURDLED, AND THE NEXT MOMENT HE WAS IN IT.

EGGS BENEDICT?

PRECISELY.

THAT WAS A MONTH AGO, AND I HAVEN'T EATEN PROPERLY SINCE. WHOEVER MURDERED OSCAR INTENDS TO DO THE SAME TO ME.

WHAT DID THE POLICE FIND?

THE POLICE? HA! THEY DIDN'T BELIEVE ME. THEY SAID POOR OSCAR DROPPED DEAD FROM A BUM HEART.

DID OSCAR *HAVE* A BUM HEART?

HE MOST CERTAINLY DID BY THE TIME *THEY* SAW IT.

NO TRACES OF POISON WERE FOUND?

NO, BUT THE DOCTOR SAYS THERE ARE SEVERAL TYPES OF POISON THAT MIGHT NOT BE FOUND.

HE'S RIGHT. DO YOU HAVE ANY IDEA WHO MIGHT HAVE--

YOU WOULDN'T HAVE ANOTHER ONE OF THOSE DELICIOUS *SANDWICHES*, WOULD YOU?

NOT ON ME.

THEN LET'S DISCUSS THE DETAILS OVER LUNCH. I'M *FAMISHED*.

"I WAS ALL FOR A CELEBRATION. NOT ONLY WAS I STARVING, BUT I WAS $2,100.00 RICHER THAN I'D BEEN TEN MINUTES AGO. AND THIS CASE WOULD BE A CINCH."

"MABLE WINGATE WAS IN NO DANGER OF BEING POISONED. HER LATE HUSBAND HAD BEEN DROPPED BY A BAD TICKER.

"IT HAD BEEN GOOD ENOUGH FOR THE COPS, AND IT WAS GOOD ENOUGH FOR ME. THERE WAS NO CRIME.

"MABLE'S MIND HAD INVENTED A MURDER PLOT TO HELP HER COPE WITH THE SHOCK OF OSCAR'S DEATH. DOCTORS HAVE A NAME FOR THAT. SO DO I--BANANAS.

"MABLE WAS BANANAS. AND RICH! I STOOD TO MAKE OUT LIKE A BANDIT."

I'M NOT BIG ON JAPANESE FOOD.

NONETHELESS, I AM. I JUST *ADORE* SUSHI.

WHO'S SUSHI? THE WAITRESS?

YAMAMOI
FINE JAPANESE CUISINE

YOU HAVE A LOT TO LEARN, DUKE.

"SHE ORDERED THE SAME MEAL FOR BOTH OF US."

YAMAMOTO
FINE JAPANESE

ONE OF MY RELATIVES IS CLEARLY THE *VILLAIN*. WITH OSCAR GONE, THE FAMILY FORTUNE FELL INTO MY HANDS. ONCE I'M OUT OF THE WAY, THEY'LL INHERIT *OODLES*.

WHO, EXACTLY, WILL GET THE OODLES?

57

WHAT *IS* THIS STUFF?

SUSHI, MY DEAR.

IT LOOKS LIKE *DEAD FISH!*

"MABLE GIGGLED. THE LAST TIME I'D SMELLED SOMETHING LIKE THIS, I WAS A KID IN A ROWBOAT GRABBING BAIT FROM A BUCKET."

I'M NOT GOING TO EAT THIS.

Oh, BUT YOU MUST. UNTIL YOU CATCH THE KILLER, YOU'LL HAVE TO BE MY *FOOD TASTER.*

WHAT ARE YOU GETTING AT?

EAT!

"FOR THREE HUNDRED DOLLARS A DAY, I'LL EAT ANYTHING.

"IT TASTED THE WAY I WAS AFRAID IT WOULD.

58

"AFTER LEAVING YAMA-MOTO'S SUSHI BAR AND BAIT SHOP, WE TOOK THE LIMO TO WINGATE MANOR."

"MABLE INTRODUCED ME AS THE SON OF AN OLD SCHOOL CHUM, DOWN ON HIS LUCK, WHO'D BE LIVING IN FOR A WEEK. I DIDN'T COMPLAIN-- THE PLACE WAS LIKE A LUXURY HOTEL."

"NO WONDER HER TWO DAUGH-TERS, HER SON, AND THEIR ASSORTED MATES WEREN'T EAGER TO MOVE OUT.

"AT COCKTAIL HOUR I ORDERED A SCOTCH, BUT GOT A VODKA MARTINI--SAME AS MABLE. AFTER I TOOK A SIP, WE SWITCHED GLASSES WITHOUT ANYONE NOTICING. "

"NONE OF THEM STRUCK ME AS KILLERS. THAT WAS NO SUR-PRISE, SINCE I'D DECIDED THAT MABLE'S DECK WAS A FEW CARDS SHORT.

60

"GEORGE, THE BUTLER, PASSED AROUND MINIATURE SANDWICHES THAT MABLE CALLED CANAPES."

AS OUR GUEST, WHY DON'T YOU HELP YOURSELF FIRST, DUKE?

"IT HAD LIVER INSIDE. I'M NOT BIG ON LIVER, BUT IT SURE BEATS SUSHI.

"WHEN I DIDN'T KEEL OVER, MABLE TOOK ONE. THEN DINNER WAS SERVED, AND I STARTED TO HEAD FOR A JUICY-SMELLING ROAST, WHEN MABLE GRABBED ME."

DUKE AND I WILL BE DINING LATER. WE HAVE SOME THINGS TO DISCUSS.

I CAN'T LET THEM SEE THAT I'VE HIRED A FOOD TASTER. THEN, I'D KNOW I'M ON TO THEIR GAME.

"BANANAS, FOR SURE. AND I COULD'VE USED A FEW BANANAS JUST THEN. I WAS STARVING, BUT WE HAD TO WAIT UNTIL EVERYONE CHOWED DOWN.

"FINALLY, THE DINING ROOM CLEARED, AND IT WAS OUR TURN. THE ROAST WAS COLD, BUT DELICIOUS. I TOOK A BIG BITE. MABLE WATCHED AND WAITED.

61

"I POURED GRAVY OVER THE MASHED POTATOES, AND TOOK A BIG BITE. SHE RAISED HER EYEBROW. I SIPPED WINE. I ATE A YUCKY CHUNK OF BROCCOLI. SHE KEPT STARING."

HOW ARE YOU FEELING?

STARVED.

YOU'RE DOING SPLENDIDLY!

"WE TRADED PLATES AND GLASSES. THIS WENT ON AT EVERY MEAL FOR FIVE DAYS. EXCEPT FOR ONE RETURN TRIP TO YAMAMOTO'S, IT WASN'T HALF BAD."

"I SPENT MY DAYS SWIMMING, RIDING HORSES, AND PLAYING TENNIS. MABLE'S SON-IN-LAW, AARON, SHOWED A NASTY STREAK ON THE COURTS."

"HE LIKED TO SLAM BALLS AT MY FACE. HE WAS A DOCTOR WHEN HE WASN'T HANGING AROUND THE ESTATE. IF I HAD TO PICK A LIKELY POISONER, IT WOULD'VE BEEN HIM."

"BUT I DIDN'T HAVE TO PICK. NOBODY HAD ANY INTENTION OF POISONING MABLE.

"SHE DIDN'T NEED A PRIVATE EYE OR A FOOD TASTER. SHE NEEDED A HEAD DOCTOR. I KNEW THAT ALL ALONG.

"I PRIED OPEN ONE OF THE SNACKS AND SNIFFED IT."

LIVER. YUCK!

"I TOSSED IT ACROSS THE KITCHEN.

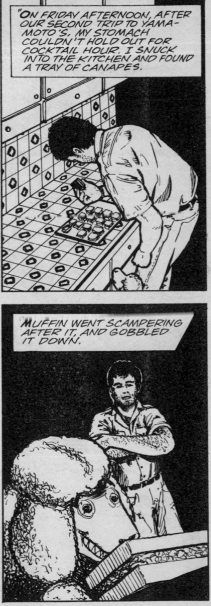

"ON FRIDAY AFTERNOON, AFTER OUR SECOND TRIP TO YAMAMOTO'S, MY STOMACH COULDN'T HOLD OUT FOR COCKTAIL HOUR. I SNUCK INTO THE KITCHEN AND FOUND A TRAY OF CANAPES.

MUFFIN WENT SCAMPERING AFTER IT, AND GOBBLED IT DOWN.

"ADIOS, MUFFIN. THE CANAPE WAS POISONED. MABLE WASN'T BANANAS AFTER ALL!"

"THAT MADE ME FEEL GOOD. I'D GROWN FOND OF THE OLD DAME AND WAS GLAD TO FIND OUT SHE WASN'T A LOONY."

"I RETURNED THE POISONED SNACKS TO THE REFRIGERATOR AND STASHED THE REMAINS OF MUFFIN IN THE PANTRY. THEN I WENT TO FETCH SLUGGER, MY .38 CALIBER REVOLVER."

"BY FIVE O'CLOCK, THE WHOLE GANG WAS OUT AT THE POOL."

HAS ANYONE SEEN MUFFIN?

"NOBODY HAD, INCLUDING ME."

"THE BUTLER BROUGHT DRINKS. I SIPPED MINE. THEN MABLE TRIED TO SWITCH GLASSES, BUT I STOPPED HER."

NOT NECESSARY.

QUIET! DUKE IS A PRIVATE DETECTIVE WHOM I'VE HIRED TO PROTECT ME.

"THAT SHUT THEM UP. SOME LOOKED SURPRISED, OTHERS CONFUSED. A FEW WERE ANGRY.

"AARON LOOKED MORE ANGRY THAN ANYONE. I WAS GLAD HE DIDN'T HAVE A TENNIS RACKET HANDY."

ALL OF YOU--LINE UP!

WHAT IS THE MEANING OF THIS?

YOU'LL SOON FIND OUT. MABLE--THE *TRAY*.

ONE CANAPÉ APIECE.

"SHE WALKED SLOWLY PAST THE ELEVEN SUSPECTS, HANDING EACH ONE OF THEM A LITTLE SANDWICH."

OKAY, WHEN I COUNT TO THREE, I WANT YOU ALL TO EAT YOUR SNACKS.

67

"AARON FROZE. THE OTHER TEN DIDN'T. THEY DROPPED. SOME PITCHED ONTO THE CONCRETE. SOME FLOPPED INTO THE POOL."

YOU IDIOT!

OH, BOY...

"IN THIS GAME, SOME CASES ARE TOUGH. SOME ARE A LEAD-PIPE CINCH. YOU WIN A FEW AND YOU LOSE A FEW. YOU HOPE IT ALL EVENS OUT IN THE END, BUT IF IT DOESN'T...WELL, THAT'S THE WAY THE COOKIE CRUMBLES.

"I WOULDN'T HAVE IT ANY OTHER WAY. I'M A SLEUTH, A SNOOP, A GUMSHOE. I'M THE GUY YOU CALL WHEN THE CHIPS ARE DOWN AND YOUR BACK'S TO THE WALL. I'M DUKE SCANLON, PRIVATE EYE."

EATS

by
Richard Laymon

Born in Chicago, Richard Laymon is a graduate of Willamette University in Oregon and Loyola University in Los Angeles. He currently lives in Los Angeles with his wife and his daughter. Laymon is the author of twelve horror novels, including *Flesh, Resurrection Dreams,* and *Funland.* His short stories have appeared in such anthologies as *Book of the Dead* and *Night Visions 7.*

Now that you've read this story, ask yourself:

- Would you have taken on Duke's assignment?

- What do you think of Duke's detective work?

- How would you have handled the case differently?

*W*HO?
BY
MICHAEL COLLINS

Story Adapted by Fred Schiller

Illustrated by Delfin Barral

71

THIS IS MY BOYD. HE WAS ONLY EIGHTEEN AND HEALTHY AS A HORSE. HE'D JUST PASSED THE PHYSICAL FOR JOINING THE AIR FORCE.

SHE TOLD ME THAT BOYD RAN WITH A STREET GANG CALLED THE NIGHT ANGELS AND THAT SHE THOUGHT THEY MIGHT BE INVOLVED.

SHE WAS A DES-PERATE WOMAN... I COULDN'T TURN HER DOWN.

SOMEONE TOOK MY BOY'S LIFE FROM HIM... FROM ME...

FIND THE PERSON WHO DID IT... PLEASE.

MY FIRST STOP WAS THE COUNTY MORGUE.

72

73

74

I ASKED TO SEE BOYD'S ROOM, HOPING TO FIND A CLUE TO WHAT, OR WHO, HAD KILLED HIM.

HIS DRESSER HELD THE USUAL STUFF. IT TOLD ME NOTHING.

THE ONLY INTERESTING THING I FOUND WAS UNDER THE BED.

IT WAS AN EMPTY BOTTLE OF AFTER-SHAVE -- WAY TOO EXPENSIVE FOR A KID LIKE BOYD.

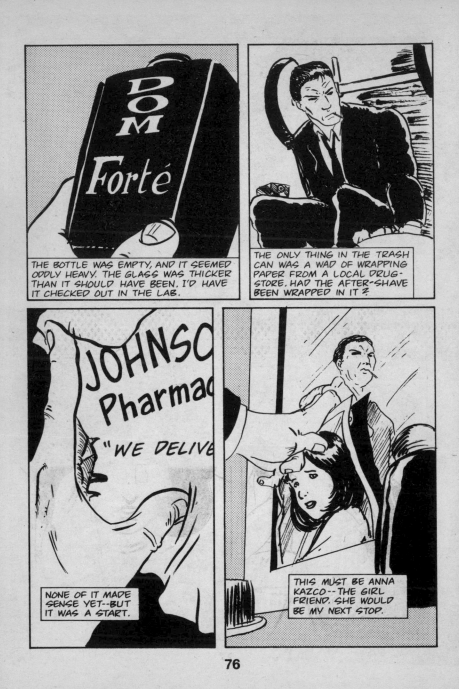

THE BOTTLE WAS EMPTY, AND IT SEEMED ODDLY HEAVY. THE GLASS WAS THICKER THAN IT SHOULD HAVE BEEN. I'D HAVE IT CHECKED OUT IN THE LAB.

THE ONLY THING IN THE TRASH CAN WAS A WAD OF WRAPPING PAPER FROM A LOCAL DRUG-STORE. HAD THE AFTER-SHAVE BEEN WRAPPED IN IT?

JOHNSO
Pharmac
"WE DELIVE

NONE OF IT MADE SENSE YET--BUT IT WAS A START.

THIS MUST BE ANNA KAZCO--THE GIRL FRIEND. SHE WOULD BE MY NEXT STOP.

I KILLED BOYD CONNORS, MR. FORTUNE-- I'M THE REASON HE'S DEAD!

BOYD WAS LEAVING ME TO JOIN THE AIR FORCE, SO I STARTED SEEING ROGER TATUM, TO MAKE BOYD JEALOUS. THE SHOCK MUST HAVE BEEN TOO MUCH FOR HIM.

I ASSURED HER THAT NO ONE HAD EVER DIED FROM A BROKEN HEART, AND ASKED FOR DETAILS OF WHAT HAD HAPPENED THE DAY BEFORE.

SHE TOLD ME THAT SHE AND ROGER HAD BEEN SITTING ON HER FRONT STOOP, WHEN CONNORS STORMED UP.

79

I PUT THE WORD OUT ON THE STREET THAT I WAS BUYING INFORMATION ON BOYD CONNORS.

I HIT PAYDIRT WHEN A MEMBER OF CONNORS' GANG, THE NIGHT ANGELS, SHOWED UP.

"THE LAST TIME ANY OF US SAW CONNORS, HE WAS WAVING THIS PACKAGE AROUND -- CLAIMING THAT THE SAP WHO LOST IT WAS IN DEEP TROUBLE."

CONNORS HAD GONE HOME RIGHT AFTER THAT... AND WAS DEAD AN HOUR LATER.

81

82

83

THE FINAL PIECES WERE FALLING INTO PLACE.

MR. PADGETT WILL SEE YOU NOW, MR. FORTUNE.

I PLAYED A HUNCH AND ASKED PADGETT IF HE HAD A BAD HEART.

WELL, YES, I DO, MR. FORTUNE -- BUT IT'S UNDER CONTROL.

STILL, IT WOULDN'T LOOK STRANGE IF YOU WERE TO DIE FROM A HEART ATTACK, RIGHT?

WHO WOULD WANT YOU DEAD, MR. PADGETT?

84

WHEN HE TOLD ME, I CALLED AND HAD A POLICE CRUISER PICK US UP. WE STOPPED AT THE DRUGSTORE AND PICKED UP ROGER TATUM'S BOSS.

WE WENT TO THE APARTMENT OF PADGETT'S PARTNER, SAMUEL SEAVER. HE WAS THE ONLY MAN WHO WOULD PROFIT FROM PADGETT'S DEATH.

YES, WHO IS IT? PADGETT? BUT I THOUGHT YOU... YOU...

3-B

TATUM'S BOSS NEARLY JUMPED OUT OF HIS SHOES WHEN HE SAW SEAVER.

THAT'S HIM! THAT'S THE MAN WHO WAS IN MY STORE YESTERDAY!

SAMUEL SEAVER, YOU ARE UNDER ARREST FOR THE MURDER OF BOYD CONNORS--

WHO?!

FOR THE MURDER OF WHO?

IT ALL MADE SENSE NOW. SEAVER HAD REPLACED THE BOTTLES OF AFTER-SHAVE, WITH ONE FULL OF NERVE GAS--GAS DESIGNED TO TRIGGER A HEART ATTACK.

CONNORS HAD TAKEN HOME THE PACKAGE THAT TATUM HAD DROPPED, HOPING TO GET THE KID IN TROUBLE. WHEN HE OPENED IT, HE NEVER KNEW WHAT HIT HIM.

WHO?
by
Michael Collins

Michael Collins is also Dennis Lynds, William Arden, Nick Carter, Maxwell Grant, and Mark Sadler, to name few of his pen names. He was born in 1924 and started his career as a chemist. He fought in the infantry in World War II and received the Bronze Star and the Purple Heart. He has gotten numerous awards for his work, including a special award by the Mystery Writers Association for his short story "Success of a Mission." Collins says, "I write because I can . . . It's my way of trying to understand the world I live in."

In "Who?" Michael Collins played detective. Now that you've read this story, ask yourself:

- Who were the possible suspects in the murder?

- Do you think the author's plot is logical?

- Can you suggest another solution to the murder? How would your idea develop?

THE STOLEN CIGAR-CASE

BY

BRET HARTE

Story Adapted and Illustrated
by Bob Versandi

89

FROM THE SQUISHING SOUND OF YOUR BOOTS UPON THE STAIRS, AND THE DRIPPING OF YOUR UMBRELLA UPON MY FLOOR.

ASTOUNDING. WHICH FACT MADE YOU CERTAIN YOU WERE CORRECT?

NEITHER. THIS STEADY SPLASHING ON MY NOGGIN WAS THE CONVINCER.

AH, NOW TELL ME-- WHAT FIENDISH CRIME CURRENTLY OCCUPIES YOUR MIND, MY FRIEND?

WHATS-ON, THERE ARE FIVE DEEDS OF VILLAINY THAT REQUIRE MY ATTENTION THIS DAY.

FIVE? PLEASE GIVE ME THE DETAILS.

PRINCE BOOPADOOP WISHES ME TO FIND A MISSING RUBY FROM THE KREMLIN. THE RAJAH OF RUTABAGA ASKS THAT I RECOVER A STOLEN GOLDEN SWORD.

THE GRAND DUCHESS OF PRETZELBENDER WANTS ME TO FIND HER MISSING HUSBAND! AND THE MAN IN THE APARTMENT BELOW IS SEEKING A LOST GLOVE.

INCREDIBLE! BUT YOU SAID FIVE CASES, AND THAT WAS FOUR.

CORRECT, OLD FRIEND! I SAVED THE LAST AND MOST HORRIFIC OF THE CRIMES FOR A MORE DETAILED DESCRIPTION.

GAD! HAS A MEMBER OF THE ROYAL FAMILY BEEN KIDNAPPED?

WORSE THAN THAT.

WORSE THAN *THAT?*

I HAVE BEEN ROBBED.

91

GOOD LORD.!

YOU RECALL THE CIGAR-CASE PRESENTED TO ME BY THE TURKISH AMBASSADOR, ALI TURIN BEY, FOR SAVING HIS SON FROM THE TUSKS OF A WILD BOAR LAST SUMMER?

THE ONE ENCRUSTED WITH DIAMONDS?

I SAW NO DIAMONDS ON THE BOAR.

I WAS SPEAKING OF THE CIGAR-CASE.

QUITE SO. THE VERY SAME. STOLEN FROM ME BY A THIEF WITHOUT SHAME OR CONSCIENCE. A CRIMINAL WITHOUT HEART OR SOUL. A SWINE WITHOUT HONOR OR DIGNITY.

HE DOES HAVE ONE THING TO HIS MERIT.

SUCH AS?

YOUR CIGAR-CASE.

92

PRECISELY WHAT I INTENDED. EXCUSE ME, OLD FRIEND, WHILE I GO AND FIND SOME WRITING PAPER IN THE NEXT ROOM TO RECORD THESE AVENUES OF ACTION!

CERTAINLY. I SHALL AMUSE MYSELF AT THE LABORATORY TABLE.

HEMLOCK JONES LEFT DR. WHATS-ON ALONE IN THE STUDY WHILE HE WENT IN SEARCH OF HIS WRITING PAD.

Hmmm, I WONDER WHAT EXPERIMENTS JONES HAS BEEN DOING WITH THESE ?

A JAR OF BELLY BUTTON LINT, A CONTAINER OF PIPE ASH, A BAG OF FINGER-NAIL CLIPPINGS, AND A BOX OF CHICKEN BONES ?

WHATS-ON FAILED TO SEE THE FIGURE OBSERVING HIS MOVEMENTS FROM THE TRANSOM ABOVE THE SITTING ROOM DOOR.

STRANGE. THE LABORATORY DRAWER HANDLES ARE COVERED WITH SOME STICKY SUBSTANCE.

94

95

96

97

98

99

YOU STOLE THE CIGAR-CASE TO PAWN IT. YOU NEEDED A LARGE SUM OF MONEY FOR A NEW SEAL-SKIN COAT.

WHAT SEAL-SKIN COAT?

THE SEAL-SKIN COAT YOU PURCHASED FOR YOUR NEW GIRL FRIEND. IT HAD TO HAVE BEEN HER EMBRACE THAT LEFT A LINE OF LOOSE HAIRS ON THE SLEEVE OF YOUR COAT YESTERDAY.

BUT I EXPLAINED THAT. I HAD BEEN TO THE BARBER.

A CLEVER BUT OBVIOUS LIE. YOUR VISITS TO THE BARBER LEAVE YOU SMELLING STRONGLY OF WITCH HAZEL, AND YESTERDAY YOU DID NOT SMELL.

BE SENSIBLE, SIR. THE RAIN MUST HAVE WASHED IT AWAY.

I ALSO TOOK THE OPPORTUNITY TO MEASURE YOUR ARM WHEN I SHOWED YOU THE SEAL-SKIN HAIRS. AND THE LENGTH OF YOUR ARM MATCHED THE DISTANCE FROM YOUR CHAIR TO THE DRAWER FROM WHICH THE CIGAR-CASE WAS TAKEN.

101

102

DR. WHATS-ON EXAMINED THE PARTIALLY OPENED DRAWER OF HEMLOCK JONES' LABORATORY TABLE.

IT APPEARS THERE IS SOMETHING STUCK AT THE REAR OF THE DRAWER.

AN ELEMENTARY CONCLUSION, WHATS-ON.

HELLO? I SEEMED TO HAVE FREED THE OBSTRUCTION?

WELL?

WELL, WELL, WELL. LOOK AT WHAT I FOUND.

MY CIGAR-CASE!

WHAT DO YOU SAY NOW, JONES?

A NASTY BIT OF TRICKERY, WHICH MIGHT HAVE FOOLED ANY-ONE BUT MYSELF!

WHAT?

IT IS OBVIOUS. FEARING MY DISCOVERY OF YOUR CRIMINAL ACTS, YOU STOLE THE CIGAR-CASE BACK FROM THE PAWNBROKER. YESTERDAY, YOU HID IT AT THE BACK OF THE DRAWER WHEN I LEFT THE ROOM.

WHAAAAAAT?

YOU PRETENDED TO "FIND" THE CIGAR-CASE TODAY TO AVOID ARREST AND RUIN. I SHALL FORGET THE ENTIRE EPISODE...IF YOU PROMISE TO RETURN TO THE PRACTICE OF MEDICINE AND NEVER STRAY AGAIN.

I NEVER SAW HEMLOCK JONES AGAIN. AS A RESULT, MY MEDICAL PRACTICE FLOURISHED. I BECAME RICH AND RESPECTED. YET, SO CONVINCING WAS HE, THAT WHENEVER I CHANCE TO RECALL OUR LAST MEETING... I SOMETIMES WONDER IF PERHAPS I MIGHT HAVE TAKEN HIS CIGAR-CASE AFTER ALL!

J. WHATS·ON

104

THE STOLEN CIGAR-CASE

by
Bret Harte

Francis Brett Harte was born in Albany, New York, in 1839. He had little formal education but was a great reader. His favorite author was Charles Dickens, who influenced Harte's writing enormously. He worked on a newspaper for a while and it was at this time that he began using the signature Bret Harte. In 1868 he was appointed editor of a frontier magazine called *The Overland Monthly*. His most famous stories, ''The Luck of Roaring Camp'' and ''The Outcasts of Poker Flat,'' were written for this magazine, and established his reputation as a writer of colorful stories of frontier life.

''The Stolen Cigar-Case'' is a comic spoof done in the style of Arthur Conan Doyle, creator of Sherlock Holmes.

Now that you've read this story, ask yourself:

- Do you think Harte did a good job in catching the flavor of the Sherlock stories?

- Did Hemlock Jones's deductions remind you of the great detective?

- Do you like reading spoofs of this kind? Why or why not?

THE DISAPPEARING MAN

BY
ISAAC ASIMOV

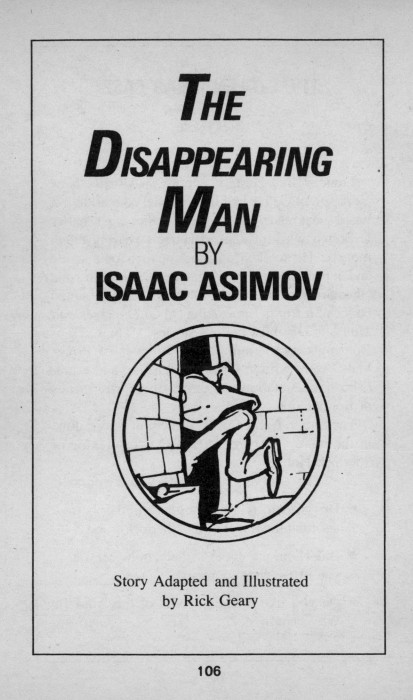

Story Adapted and Illustrated
by Rick Geary

"I'M NOT OFTEN ON THE SPOT WHEN DAD'S ON ONE OF HIS CASES, BUT I COULDN'T HELP IT THIS TIME."

109

IF THAT'S WHO IT IS, THERE'S LIABLE TO BE SOME SHOOTING. YOU'D BETTER GET ON HOME.

BUT, DAD...

YOU HEARD ME -- HOME!

"BUT I DIDN'T GO HOME. I JUST DUCKED AROUND THE CORNER -- I WANTED TO DO SOME THINKING."

NOBODY LEAVES ALLEY DOORS OPEN IN NEW YORK. IF THAT DOOR WAS FOUND OPEN, STOCKTON MUST HAVE A KEY -- BECAUSE THERE WASN'T TIME TO PICK THE LOCK. AND IF HE HAD A KEY TO THE DOOR, IT PROBABLY MEANS HE WORKS IN THE BUILDING.

"IT WAS AN OLD OFFICE BUILDING -- JUST FOUR STORIES HIGH."

111

"I COULD SEE THE PAINTED SIGNS OF BUSINESSES ON THE WINDOWS. ON THE TOP FLOOR WAS A JEWELER. IT OCCURED TO ME THAT PERHAPS THE THIEF WANTED TO USE THAT JEWELER AS HIS 'FENCE' TO SELL THE STOLEN GOODS.

"I WAITED FOR THE SOUND OF SHOTS, HOPING DAD WOULDN'T GET HURT. BUT NOTHING HAPPENED.

"AFTER A WHILE I GOT TIRED OF WAITING."

THEY MUST HAVE HIM IN CUSTODY BY NOW.

"I THOUGHT IT WAS ALL OVER, AND I WAS VERY CURIOUS. SO I CAREFULLY AVOIDED THE POLICE AND WALKED BACK TO THE BUILDING'S FRONT ENTRANCE."

DAD'LL BE HOPPING MAD—BUT I HAVE TO FIND OUT WHAT HAPPENED!

114

115

BUT HE *DID* GO IN. THERE HE IS! THAT MAN THERE!

"*THE MAN I POINTED OUT--IN A POLICEMAN'S UNIFORM-- MADE A DASH FOR THE DOOR.*

"*BUT HE WAS GRABBED AND IDENTIFIED. BINGO! IT WAS STOCKTON!*

"LATER, WHEN DAD GOT HOME, HE HAD SOME THINGS TO SAY ABOUT ME RISKING MY LIFE... BUT I COULD TELL HE WAS PROUD."

YOU CAUGHT ON TO HIS POLICE COSTUME PRETTY FAST, SON.

AT FIRST I THOUGHT HE'D GONE TO THE JEWELERS. BUT HE KNEW THE BUILDING WOULD BE SEARCHED, SO HE BROKE INTO THE COSTUME SHOP INSTEAD. THAT'S WHAT I WOULD'VE DONE, ANYWAY.

THEY WERE BOUND TO HAVE POLICE UNIFORMS, AND IF HE COULD DUMP HIS SHIRT AND PANTS AND GET INTO ONE QUICKLY, HE COULD JUST **WALK** OUT OF THE BUILDING.

118

THE DISAPPEARING MAN
by
Isaac Asimov

Isaac Asimov was born in 1920. His father owned a candy store, and Asimov loved to read "Amazing Stories" and the pulp magazines his father sold in the store. But his father thought they were "trash" and forbade it. It was only after he convinced his dad that some of the stories had "science" in them that he was allowed to read them.

Now Asimov is one of the most powerful forces in his field. Asimov's story "Nightfall" (*Nightfall and Other Stories*, Doubleday 1969) was chosen as the best science fiction story of all time in a poll taken by the Science Fiction Writers of America.

In "The Disappearing Man," the hero is a boy who helps his father solve crimes. Now that you've read this story, ask yourself:

- What was the first clue the author planted?

- Did you guess how the boy figured out who Stockton was?

- Why do you think Asimov made the boy the hero of this story?

THE LITTLE OLD LADY FROM CRICKET CREEK

BY
LEN GRAY

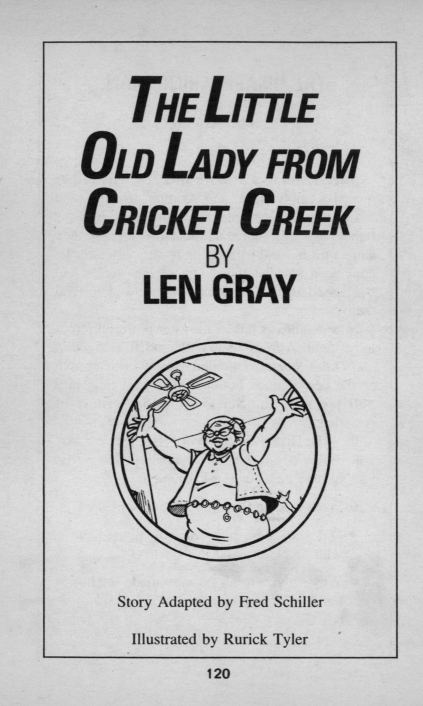

Story Adapted by Fred Schiller

Illustrated by Rurick Tyler

"ART BOWDEN AND I WERE REVIEWING THE EMPLOYEE FILES WHEN PENNY, OUR SECRETARY, POPPED HER HEAD IN THE DOOR.

GREAT RIVEROAKS INSURANCE COMPANY.

"ART AND I RUN THE PERSONNEL DEPARTMENT OF THE GREAT RIVEROAKS INSURANCE COMPANY. THAT MEANS WE HIRE AND FIRE PEOPLE."

EXCUSE ME, MR. CUMMINGS. THERE'S A MRS. MABEL JUMPSTONE HERE APPLYING FOR THE FILE CLERK JOB. AND, SIR, SHE'S... WELL, SHE'S... OLD!

ANYONE OVER TWENTY-FIVE IS OLD TO YOU, PENNY. LET'S TAKE A LOOK AT MRS. JUMPSTONE'S APPLICATION. HUH! FIFTY-FIVE! MAYBE SHE IS A LITTLE OLD FOR THE JOB.

121

123

124

THE NEXT DAY...

WELL, PARTNER, WHAT'S THE WORD ON OUR TYPING WHIZ?

PERSO

SHE CHECKS OUT FINE, ART. I JUST CALLED HER, AND SHE STARTS TOMORROW.

THE OTHER CLERKS ARE GOING TO CHOKE ON THEIR CHEWING GUM WHEN THEY SEE HER. THIS COULD BE INTERESTING...

"ART HAD NO IDEA OF JUST HOW INTER-ESTING."

128

"SHE ALWAYS SENT A CARD AND FLOWERS, OR VISITED WHEN SOMEONE WAS SICK.

GET WELL SOON

"BEFORE LONG, PEOPLE STARTED COMING TO MABEL WITH THEIR PERSONAL PROBLEMS.

"AND SHE ALWAYS FOUND A WAY TO HELP THEM OUT."

129

130

"THE POLICE WANTED HER APPLICATION, TO GET HER HOME ADDRESS. BUT IT WAS MISSING. ALL WE FOUND IN THE FILE WAS A TYPED RESIGNATION. ALL WE REMEMBERED WAS THAT SHE WAS FROM CRICKET CREEK, CALIFORNIA.

"THE POLICE TRIED NOT TO LAUGH AT US. THEY EVEN GAVE ME A RIDE HOME TO MY APARTMENT.

"AS IT TURNED OUT, THERE WAS NO CRICKET CREEK.

131

"THE BIG BOSSES WOULD BE UPSET FOR A WHILE. BUT BEFORE LONG IT WOULD ALL BLOW OVER. I FIGURED THAT I WOULD TAKE SOME VACATION TIME UNTIL IT DID.

"MONEY WASN'T A PROBLEM ANYMORE."

I HOPE YOU WIPED YOUR FEET BEFORE YOU CAME IN! YOUR DINNER'S IN THE OVEN. NOW DON'T INTERRUPT ME--I'M COUNTING!

YES, MOTHER.

BOSSY & MILK
MOO MOO GOOD!

THE LITTLE OLD LADY FROM CRICKET CREEK
by
Len Gray

Len Gray was a pen name for the late mystery author Albert B. Ralston. He also wrote under the name Trevor Black. Ralston mainly wrote short mystery stories, many of which were published in *Alfred Hitchcock's Mystery Magazine*. Two of his better-known mystery stories were "Albert and the Amateurs" and "A Matter of Routine."

In "The Little Old Lady from Cricket Creek," we find out that even sweet elderly people can be thieves at heart.

Now that you've read this story, ask yourself:

- Do you think the robbery was Ralph's idea, or his mother's?

- Did Mrs. Jumpstone do anything to make you think she was a thief?

- Do you think that Ralph will continue to work for the company? Why, or why not?

THE OBLONG BOX
BY
EDGAR ALLAN POE

Story Adapted and Illustrated
by John Pierard

"SEVERAL YEARS AGO, I HAD THE MOST HORRIBLE EXPERIENCE AT SEA. IT HAUNTS ME TO THIS DAY. I SHALL TELL YOU THE STORY... AND PERHAPS IT WILL HELP TO LESSEN THE HORROR.

"I HAD ARRANGED TO TRAVEL FROM MY HOME IN SOUTH CAROLINA TO NEW YORK CITY. I BOOKED PASSAGE ON THE GOOD SHIP INDEPENDENCE-- A THREE-MASTED SCHOONER, SWIFT AND SOUND."

"THE DAY BEFORE WE WERE TO SAIL, I WENT ON BOARD TO ARRANGE SOME MATTERS.

"AS I SIGNED THE REGISTER, I WAS HAPPY TO NOTE THAT AMONG THE PASSENGERS WAS MY DEAR FRIEND, MR. CORNELIUS WYATT, A FINE ARTIST."

HMMM. WYATT IS SAILING WITH HIS NEW BRIDE AND HIS TWO SISTERS. YET, HE'S BOOKED THREE ROOMS RATHER THAN TWO. HOW ODD... MUST BE FOR EXTRA BAGGAGE.

"WYATT HAD PLANNED TO MEET ME THAT DAY TO INTRODUCE ME TO HIS WIFE. HOWEVER, HE SENT A NOTE INSTEAD, SAYING THAT MRS. W. WAS ILL. SHE WOULD NOT GO OUT UNTIL JUST BEFORE SAILING.

"THE NEXT DAY I WAS QUITE EXCITED TO SEE THEM...

"...BUT WAS SURPRISED TO FIND THEM SO QUIET AND SAD.

EVEN WYATT'S SISTERS... SO GRIM.

"REMEMBERING THE EXTRA STATE-ROOM, I WATCHED THEIR BAGGAGE BEING LOADED. THE LAST PIECE WAS AN OBLONG PINE BOX... VERY STRANGE."

137

"WYATT'S SISTER MARION INTRODUCED ME TO HIS BRIDE. WYATT HAD MENTIONED HER GREAT BEAUTY TO ME..."

".. SO MY SURPRISE WAS GREAT WHEN SHE RAISED HER VEIL. SHE WAS QUITE PLAIN -- IF NOT DOWNRIGHT UGLY."

PLEASED TO MEET YA.

"A SHORT TIME LATER, WE SET SAIL FOR NEW YORK."

"I COULD NOT HELP BUT BE CURIOUS ABOUT THE OBLONG BOX."

IT'S ABOUT SIX FEET LONG, BY TWO AND A HALF WIDE.

"I THOUGHT IT MUST HOLD A PAINTING--AN EXPENSIVE ONE, TO BE CRATED SO CAREFULLY. IT WAS ADDRESSED TO HIS WIFE'S MOTHER.

"THE STRONG, FOUL ODOR COMING FROM IT I THOUGHT MUST BE DUE TO THE TAR OR PAINT USED TO WRITE THE ADDRESS.

"THE ODDEST THING WAS THAT IT WAS TO BE PLACED IN WYATT'S OWN ROOM--NOT THE EXTRA STATEROOM, AS I HAD THOUGHT."

"THE SUN SHONE BRIGHTLY OUR FIRST FEW DAYS, AND EVERYONE ENJOYED THE VOYAGE... EXCEPT FOR WYATT. HE KEPT MOSTLY TO HIMSELF.

"BUT THE NEW MRS. WYATT WAS QUITE SOCIABLE AND CHATTY.

"SHE AMUSED THE WOMEN... AND EVEN FLIRTED WITH THE MEN.

"BUT I SOON REALIZED THE TRUTH OF THE MATTER..."

THEY ARE ALL LAUGHING AT HER... NOT WITH HER.

"ONE DAY I SAW WYATT WALKING THE DECK BY HIMSELF. AN AIR OF GLOOM STILL SURROUNDED HIM."

WYATT, HERE YOU ARE! COME--LET US TALK.

"I WANTED TO TALK WITH HIM ABOUT THE BOX... TO SEE IF MY GUESS AS TO ITS CONTENTS WAS CORRECT."

WYATT...IT'S SUCH AN ODDLY SHAPED BOX THAT YOU'VE TAK'EN ABOARD. BUT YOU CAN'T FOOL ME. I'VE FIGURED IT OUT.

"THE WAY IN WHICH WYATT REACTED TO MY INNOCENT REMARK CONVINCED ME THAT HE WAS QUITE MAD."

"TWO SEAMEN HELPED CARRY WYATT TO HIS ROOM... AND I DETERMINED TO STAY AWAY FROM HIM FOR THE REST OF THE VOYAGE.

"HIS WIDE-EYED SCREAMS OF LAUGHTER STOPPED SHORT... AND WYATT FELL.

"THAT NIGHT AND THE NEXT, I KEPT MY CABIN DOOR OPEN BECAUSE OF THE HEAT. FROM MY BED I COULD SEE THE DOOR TO WYATT'S ROOM... AND THE STRANGE THINGS THAT OCCURRED.

"MRS. WYATT STOLE QUIETLY FROM THEIR ROOM...

"AT 11 O'CLOCK, AFTER EVERYONE HAD GONE TO BED...

"...AND ENTERED THE EXTRA CABIN, WHERE SHE STAYED THE REST OF THE NIGHT."

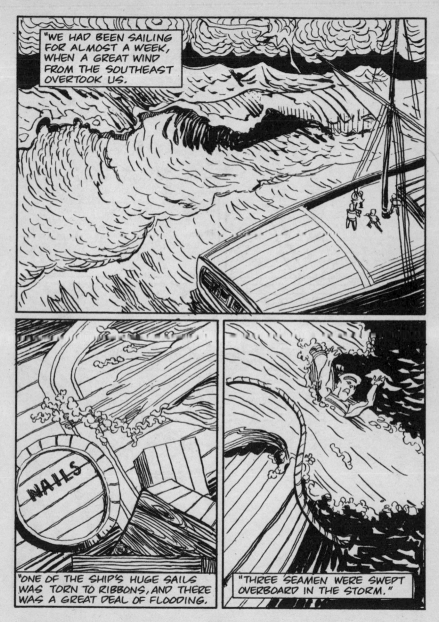

"WE HAD BEEN SAILING FOR ALMOST A WEEK, WHEN A GREAT WIND FROM THE SOUTHEAST OVERTOOK US.

"ONE OF THE SHIP'S HUGE SAILS WAS TORN TO RIBBONS, AND THERE WAS A GREAT DEAL OF FLOODING.

"THREE SEAMEN WERE SWEPT OVERBOARD IN THE STORM."

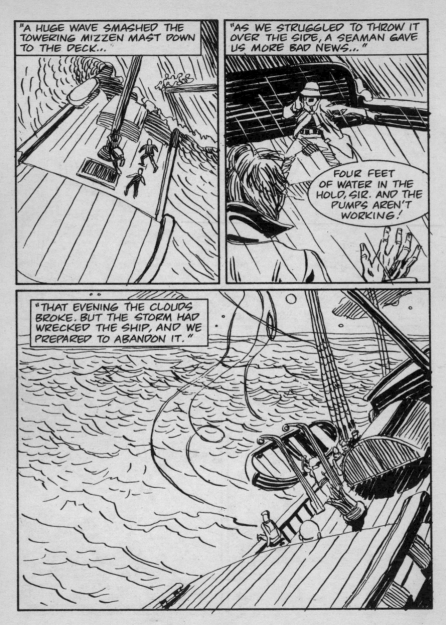

145

"THE STORM-TOSSED WATERS CARRIED US FAR FROM THE SHIP. STILL, WE COULD SEE THAT THE MAD ARTIST HAD MANAGED TO RETRIEVE THE OBLONG BOX.

"WE WATCHED, AMAZED, AS HE TIED HIMSELF TO IT WITH A STOUT ROPE. AN INSTANT LATER, BOTH DISAPPEARED UNDER THE SEA."

DID YOU SEE, CAPTAIN, HOW QUICKLY THEY SANK?

THEY WILL RISE AGAIN, HOWEVER... AS SOON AS THE SALT MELTS!

"I ASKED WHAT HE MEANT. BUT HE POINTED TO THE DEAD MAN'S SISTERS IN OUR BOAT, AND SAID THIS WAS NOT THE TIME TO DISCUSS IT."

146

"AFTER FOUR DAYS, WE LANDED SAFELY ON THE SHORES OF VIRGINIA.

"HERE WE REMAINED FOR A WEEK. FINALLY, I WAS ABLE TO BOOK ANOTHER PASSAGE TO NEW YORK.

"ABOUT A MONTH LATER, I CHANCED TO MEET CAPTAIN HARDY WHILE WALKING ON BROADWAY.

"HERE WAS MY CHANCE TO DISCUSS THE SAD FATE OF POOR WYATT."

147

"WYATT WAS DETERMINED TO MAKE THE TRIP--IF ONLY TO TAKE MRS. W'S REMAINS TO HER MOTHER."

"HARDY TOLD ME THAT WYATT DID MARRY A BEAUTIFUL WOMAN. BUT SHE HAD TAKEN ILL AND DIED THE DAY BEFORE OUR VOYAGE."

"BUT HE KNEW THE SAILORS' COMMON FEAR ABOUT SAILING WITH A CORPSE--THEY WOULD NEVER ALLOW IT."

"IT WAS HIS WIFE'S MAID WHO PLAYED MRS. WYATT. THAT EXPLAINED WHY SHE LEFT HIS CABIN EACH NIGHT... AND WHY AN EXTRA ROOM WAS NEEDED."

"THE CORPSE IN THE OBLONG BOX WAS COVERED WITH SALT, TO PRESERVE THE BODY."

"THE ONLY THING LEFT TO SAY IS THAT OF LATE I DON'T SLEEP WELL. I AM HAUNTED BY A MADDENING, GHOSTLY LAUGH, WHICH RINGS FOREVER IN MY EARS."

THE OBLONG BOX
by
Edgar Allan Poe

Edgar Allan Poe was born in the beginning of the nineteenth century. He was orphaned when he was quite young, and taken into the house of a childless couple. For a while he lived the life of a rich boy, but as he grew older, his foster parents seemed unwilling to adopt or support him.

The rest of his life was filled with problems. He was poor most of the time. For his most famous poem, "The Raven," he was paid ten dollars. Poe gambled, and had fits of depression. But he was a brilliant writer and editor, and today he is recognized as one of the all-time great writers of mystery stories.

Now that you've read this story, ask yourself:

- How does the author create a gloomy mood?

- Were you surprised at the outcome of this story? Why or why not?

- Do you think the ship was doomed because of the corpse it carried?

THE CURSE OF THE EGYPTIAN TOMB
BY
NANCY ROBERTS

Story Adapted and Illustrated
by Frederic Lere

151

FOR SIX MONTHS, ANNE PUT UP WITH THE BORING CONVERSATION OF GEORGE-TOWN'S RICH YOUNG MEN...

THIS DROUGHT HAS DONE IN OUR RICE AND COTTON. A WHOLE YEAR'S CROP TURNED TO DUST.

OUR TOBACCO HAS SUFFERED, TOO. AND PROFITS ARE DOWN ALL OVER THE COUNTRYSIDE. PERHAPS WE NEED TO PLANT SOMETHING HARDIER...

ANNE COULD NO LONGER BE POLITE. HER HEART WAS FILLED WITH LONGING FOR HER BELOVED CAPTAIN CHRISTOPHER.

GENTLEMEN, YOU BORE ME SO.

I BEG YOUR PARDON?

Ah... NO MATTER. MY CHRISTOPHER COMES BACK THIS WEEK. WE WILL BE MARRIED.

WELL, ANNE, IF YOU REALLY WANT TO MARRY THAT NOBODY...

ANNE'S FATHER WAS TRUE TO HIS PROMISE. DURING THAT WEEK, THE BEST DRESS-MAKERS OF CHARLESTON, AND THE BEST COOKS OF GEORGETOWN, WORKED TO CREATE THE FINEST WEDDING EVER SEEN IN SOUTH CAROLINA.

154

155

156

157

158

THE CURSE OF THE EGYPTIAN TOMB
by
Nancy Roberts

Nancy Roberts-Brown is best known for her books on ghosts all over the United States. But she has written books on other subjects as well. One of her most acclaimed works is *Where Time Stood Still: A Portrait of Appalachia,* which was selected as one of the outstanding books for young people in 1970 by both the *School Library Journal* and *The New York Times.* When not writing, she is busy fulfilling speaking engagements and selecting books for her catalogue collections of Southern and regional books and learning materials.

In "The Curse of the Egyptian Tomb," we never learn who cursed the ancient bracelet. But we see what happens to the young bride who wears it.

Now that you've read this story, ask yourself:

- Is there a "hero" in this story? If so, who is it?

- What do you think about the idea of objects with curses on them? Do you think it could happen?

- Do you carry any kind of lucky charm? If so, do you feel it brings you good luck?

THE GOOD TIMES ALWAYS END
BY
DAVID MORRELL

Story Adapted by Fred Schiller

Illustrated by Sterling Brown

161

"I COULDN'T REALLY BLAME MOM. SHE'D LIVED IN AND RULED THAT HOUSE FOR 60 YEARS.
SHE'D GIVEN BIRTH TO ALL SIX OF US THERE. SHE'D RAISED US THERE. MY DAD DIED IN THAT HOUSE. NOW, SHE LIVED THERE ALONE."

I KNOW, MOM. BUT THEY'RE SERIOUS. YOU'RE GOING TO HAVE TO LEAVE.

THE SHERIFF CALLED ME WHEN HE GOT BACK TO TOWN, MOM. DID YOU REALLY TEAR UP THE EVICTION NOTICE AND THROW IT IN HIS FACE?

HE WASN'T NICE TO ME AT ALL, CHARLIE. I HOPE HE DOESN'T COME BACK.

"HE'D BE BACK, ALL RIGHT. WITH DEPUTIES TO DRAG HER OUT, AND A WRECKING CREW TO DEMOLISH THE PLACE.

"THE SHERIFF RETURNED A WEEK LATER, AS I KNEW HE WOULD. I RACED TO THE HOUSE TO GET MOM OUT BEFORE THE COPS WENT IN.

301-SB

"MY WIFE AND I HAD RENTED HER A PLACE IN TOWN, NEAR OUR HOUSE. IN TIME, SHE WOULD GROW TO LIKE IT. BUT FIRST I HAD TO GET HER OUT OF THERE."

162

165

166

167

168

169

171

172

THE GOOD TIMES ALWAYS END
by
David Morrell

David Morrell is a graduate of the National Outdoor Leadership School, in Lander, Wyoming. He has a graduate degree in American Literature from Pennsylvania State University, and from 1970 to 1986 was a professor of English at the University of Iowa.

Morrell's most famous book is *First Blood*, the 1972 novel in which the character of Rambo was created. His other works include *Testament, Blood Oath, Rambo—First Blood, Part II*, and *The League of Night and Fog*.

His works have been nominated for World Fantasy Awards, and in 1989 he won a Horror Writers of America award. His latest books are *Rambo III* and *Fireflies*, an account of his 15-year-old son's death from cancer.

Now that you've read this story, ask yourself:

- Why didn't Mrs. Wade want to move?

- Why do you think she set up all of those traps in the house?

- Do you think her son was angry at her? Why, or why not?

THE DIAMOND OF KALI
BY
O. HENRY

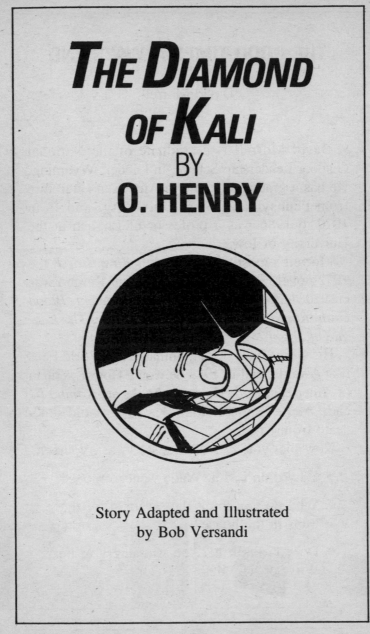

Story Adapted and Illustrated
by Bob Versandi

175

176

177

178

"I WAS IN THE JUNGLES OF SAKARANPUR, BETWEEN DELHI AND KHELAT, WHEN I CHANCED ONE NIGHT UPON A RUDE STONE TEMPLE.

"I RECOGNIZED THE TEMPLE AS ONE BELONGING TO THE BACKWARD THUGS. THEY ARE A SECRET CULT WHO STILL WORSHIP KALI, THE ANCIENT GODDESS OF DEATH. THEY PRACTICE *MURDER* AS A RELIGIOUS RITE.

"FEW HAVE EVER WITNESSED THEIR BLOODTHIRSTY CERE-MONIES AND LIVED TO TELL ABOUT IT. SO, I HID IN THE BUSHES, DETERMINED TO SEE AND SURVIVE.

"BY THE LIGHT OF A JUNGLE MOON I SOON SAW THE ARRIVAL OF HUNDREDS OF SHADOWY, CLOAKED FORMS, BEARING TORCHES AND WICKED-LOOKING KNIVES.

179

"SUDDENLY, THE DOOR OF THE TEMPLE OPENED, AND IN THE TORCHLIGHT, I SAW THE FEARSOME STATUE OF KALI. IT STOOD MORE THAN TWENTY FEET IN HEIGHT, AND WAS COVERED IN GOLD. IN THE FOREHEAD OF THE STATUE, ABOVE THE SCULPTED EYES, WAS A THIRD EYE... A DIAMOND OF BREATHTAKING SIZE AND BRILLIANCE.

"THE THUGS BEGAN A HORRIBLE CHANT, WHICH SENT SHIVERS DOWN MY SPINE. ALL AT ONCE THE CHANTING CEASED, AND THE THUGS KNELT UPON THE JUNGLE FLOOR, PUTTING THEIR FOREHEADS AGAINST THE EARTH.

"FROM BEHIND THE GOLDEN STATUE OF KALI STEPPED THE HIGH PRIEST, WHO OFFERED THE WORSHIPPERS A BLESSING FROM THE GODDESS OF DEATH.

"WHEN THE CEREMONY CONCLUDED, THE THUGS VANISHED INTO THE JUNGLE AS SILENTLY AS THEY HAD COME. ONLY THE HIGH PRIEST AND I REMAINED.

"THEN, OUT OF NOWHERE SPRANG ANOTHER FIGURE--WHO BURIED A KNIFE IN THE BACK OF THE HIGH PRIEST! AS HE COLLAPSED, THE MYSTERIOUS FIGURE SCALED THE GOLDEN IDOL, AND PRIED THE DIAMOND LOOSE FROM THE FOREHEAD OF KALI!

"WITH DIAMOND IN HAND, THE MURDERER RAN FROM THE TEMPLE INTO THE JUNGLE, DIRECTLY AT THE SPOT WHERE I HID.

"WHEN HE WAS WITHIN TWO FEET OF ME, I LET FLY AND HIT HIM BETWEEN THE EYES, KNOCKING HIM OUT INSTANTLY.

"I PICKED UP THE MAGNIFICENT JEWEL FROM WHERE IT HAD FALLEN, AND QUICKLY RETURNED TO SAKARANPUR. BY THE FOLLOWING AFTERNOON, I WAS ON MY WAY HOME WITH THE KALI DIAMOND SAFELY HIDDEN IN THE TOE OF MY BOOT."

182

183

186

MEANWHILE, UP THE STREET, THE VILLAINS CONFERRED AMONGST THEMSELVES OVER THE FLIGHT OF THEIR INTENDED VICTIMS.

HOW DID THOSE TWO KNOW THAT THE BELT SHOP IS OUTSIDE OUR GANG'S TERRITORY?

I DUNNO, BUT I WOULDN'T WANT TO HAVE BIG BILL OR *HIS* GANG FINDIN' US ON THEIR SIDE OF THE STREET. LET'S GO.

THE FOLLOWING DAY, AT THE CITY ROOM OF THE BROOKLYN BUGLE...

CONGRATULATIONS! THE KALI DIAMOND STORY CHECKED OUT AND IT RUNS ON SUNDAY.

THANKS, CHIEF.

BY THE WAY, I HEARD THAT GENERAL LUDLOW LEFT TOWN AND TOOK THE KALI DIAMOND WITH HIM. ANY NOTION AS TO WHERE HE WENT?

YEAH—HE BOUGHT A FARM IN BUCK'S COUNTY.

188

THE DIAMOND OF KALI
by
O. Henry

Born in 1862, O. Henry's real name was William Sidney Porter. He worked as a clerk, a draftsman, and finally a bank teller. He began writing stories for the newspapers and, later, for a magazine called *The Rolling Stone*. During this time something terrible happened—he was charged with embezzling funds. Porter was convicted and spent three years in prison. To support his daughter, he started writing stories. This is when he began using the name O. Henry. Known for surprise endings, O. Henry's stories are famous all over the world. Some of his best are "The Gift of the Magi" and "Alias Jimmy Valentine."

In "The Diamond of Kali," O. Henry has taken a true historical fact and shaped it into a rather comic tale.

Now that you've read this story, ask yourself:

- Does this story have a surprise ending? What is it?

- Which part of this story do you think is true? Did you check it out?

- Can you think of another "twist" ending for this story?

About the Editors

SEYMOUR V. REIT, Senior Associate Editor of the Bank Street Media Group, is author of over fifty books for children, and several non-fiction books for adults. He is also a cartoonist, and the creator of "Casper the Friendly Ghost."

BARBARA BRENNER is a writer, teacher and editor. She has written over forty books for children. Mrs. Brenner is a Senior Associate Editor with the Bank Street Media Group. She is married to illustrator Fred Brenner.

HOWARD ZIMMERMAN, a former public school teacher, is Special Projects Editor for Byron Preiss Visual Publications, Inc. He has created and edited several magazines for kids, including "Comics Scene," and has written several books on science fiction.

Share the Adventure and the Excitement of

The Bank Street Collection

Pocket Books and Bank Street, America's most trusted name in childhood education, introduce THE BANK STREET COLLECTIONS of Science Fiction, Fantasy, Creepy Tales and Mystery—graphic story comics from some of America's best cartoonists and authors.

THE BANK STREET BOOK OF SCIENCE FICTION
63145/$3.95
Authors include Andre Norton, Damon Knight, and Isaac Asimov.

THE BANK STREET BOOK OF FANTASY
63146/$3.95
Authors include H. G. Wells, Anne McCaffrey and Terry and Carol Carr.

THE BANK STREET BOOK OF CREEPY TALES
63147/$3.95
Authors include Edgar Allan Poe, and O. Henry.

THE BANK STREET BOOK OF MYSTERY
63148/$3.95
Authors include Bret Harte, Dashiell Hammett and Isaac Asimov.

Simon & Schuster Mail Order Dept. BST
200 Old Tappan Rd., Tappan, N.J. 07675

Please send me the books I have checked above. I am enclosing $_____ (please add 75¢ to cover postage and handling for each order. N.Y.S. and N.Y.C. residents please add appropriate sales tax). Send check or money order—no cash or C.O.D.'s please. Allow up to six weeks for delivery. For purchases over $10.00 you may use VISA: card number, expiration date and customer signature must be included.

Name_____

Address_____

City_____ State/Zip_____

VISA Card No._____ Exp. Date_____

Signature_____